It's Better Being a Bunny

by Marilyn Sadler

illustrated by Tim Bowers

based on characters originally illustrated by Roger Bollen

BEGINNER BOOKS®
A Division of Random House, Inc.

P. J. Funnybunny was having a bad day.
His mom would not let him eat
ice cream for breakfast.
"You could get a tummy ache," she said.

She would not let him hang
upside down from a tree.
"You could fall and hurt yourself,"
she said.

And when he wanted to see
a scary movie with Potts Pig,
she would not let him go.
"You could have a bad dream!" she said.

P.J.'s mom would not let him do *anything*.

The next day, P.J. went to Potts Pig's house to play.
His mom let him do everything.

"Can we have ice cream for lunch?"
P.J. asked Potts's mom.
"As long as you don't eat too much,"
she said.

P.J. and Potts ate two BIG bowls of
Figgy Piggy ice cream.

"Can we hang upside down from a tree?" P.J. asked.

"As long as you are careful," she said.

"If only Mom could see me now!"
shouted P.J.

"Can we go see
a scary movie today?" P.J. asked.
"As long as Polly goes with you,"
she said.
"Cool!" said P.J.
He liked Potts's sister.

P.J. was excited.

"It's better being a pig!" he said.

P.J. and Potts went to see the scariest
movie they could find.

P.J. and Potts bought two supersize popcorns.

They bought two supersize candy bars.

They bought two supersize drinks.

Then they found two seats
in the front row.
"I hope it's scary!" said P.J.

The lights dimmed. Everyone was quiet.
The movie started.

"This is spooky," whispered Potts.
"I'm not scared!" said P.J.

"Whoa!" said P.J.

"Yikes!" said Potts.

"Eeeeeeeekkk!" screamed P.J.
"Eeeeeeeekkk!" screamed Potts.

P.J. and Potts ran home
as fast as they could!

"It was a scary movie!"
Potts told his mom.
"It was *too* scary!" cried P.J.

It was time for P.J. to go home.

His mom came to pick him up.

"I ate too much ice cream, popcorn, and candy," he told her.

"You poor little bunny," she said.

That night, P.J. went to bed
with his lights on and his eyes open.

But when P.J. finally fell asleep,
he dreamed about Scary Larry!

"Eeeeeekkkk!" screamed P.J.
when he woke up.

"I had a bad dream!" P.J. cried.
Then P.J. told his mom and dad
about Scary Larry.

"I'm sorry I didn't listen to you," said P.J.

Mom and Dad tucked P.J. into bed.

He was so happy to be home!

"It was fun being a pig . . . ," said P.J.

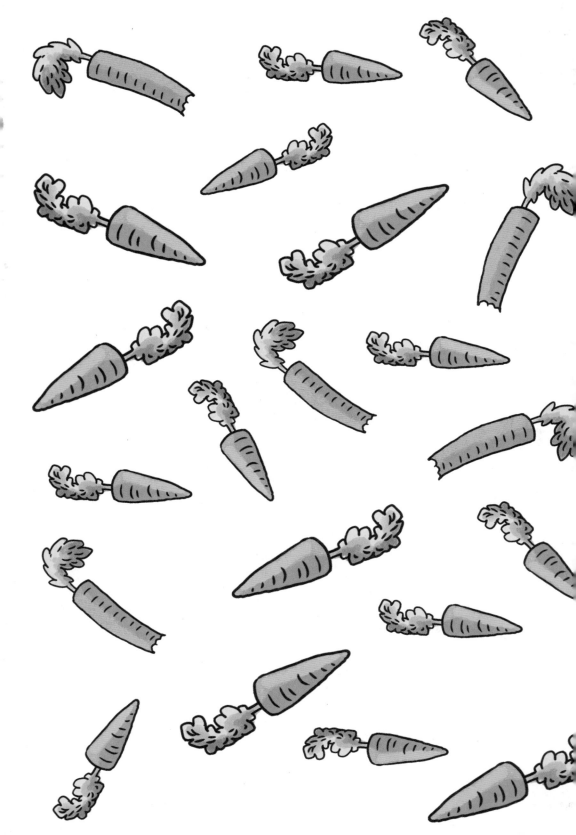